JEF

LIFERS

A micro-novel

Jeffrey Scott Weisman

LIFERS: A micro-novel

ISBN 978-1-969885-02-0

ISSN 1084-547X

The cover art is in part from "View of Fifth Block Corridor, with Gallery, two Stories high" from Richard Vaux's *Brief Sketch of the Origin and History of the State Penitentiary for the Eastern District of Pennsylvania*, 1872 (courtesy of the *Public Domain Review*). The image of the prisoners is the from the interior of Joliet State Prison circa 1890. The photographer is unknown. Courtesy of the Illinois Digital Archives, Office of the Illinois Secretary of State

This is volume 109 of
*The Journal of
Experimental Fiction*

JEF Books/Depth Charge Publishing
Arlington Heights, Illinois

"The Foremost in Innovative Fiction"
Experimentalfiction.com

LIFERS

A micro-novel

Jeffrey Scott Weisman

It is difficult to free fools from the chains they revere.

—Voltaire

For those who will follow me

HOUSES

In here, we bunk in houses. Now sure, some are covered in our families. And some are smothered in our dreams. And some are crammed with our trophies. And some are teeming with our prayers. And some are meant to impress. And some are meant to scare. And some are worthless like a condom. And some are prized like the moon. And some are valued greater than the sun. And some are even kin to the stars. But still, we all bunk in houses.

Cells, in common parlance, that is, our houses.

Jeffrey Scott Weisman

THE GENERAL ROUTINE

Wake up, piss, shit, shower (every other day at least), dress, grub, knock out my work assignment, grub yet again, hit the yard, kick through my education (on the weekdays, that is), grub one last time, dilly dally some, scribble for a bit, and crash.

And I'm lucky about that too.

What with my work assignment and all. Damn.

SETTLING SCORES

Course, as the Sunday preachers like to say, we should all turn the other cheek. Or, to quote my second cousin Gerome directly, "Let bygones be bygones." And that's not even mentioning my elementary school teacher Misses Donley who used to always end her daily lessons by stressing that "you shouldn't go casting any last stones."

But it don't work like that. At least not in this life, that is.

Jeffrey Scott Weisman

ONCE

Once I asked my pa if he was proud of me, if my aiming to pour concrete and be a finisher like him when I got done with my schooling was a proper way to carry his name cause I wanted to make him proud, being his blood and all. "I think I could really work a trowel," I said, driving home with him from the junkyard one Saturday afternoon, the corn in the fields by the junkyard knee high to a crow. "With some training and practice, I could be a man like you and work concrete. That's what I'd like to do. Ain't you proud of me?"

And he simply looked at me, his tattered baseball cap on his dome bopping back and forth as we knocked over the bumps like a bobblehead, and sniggered, "Boy, you trying to make me soil my pants or something. You ain't got a chance in hell to ever make me proud of you," a speck of spittle smacking me in the cheek.

That's right, once I asked my pa if he was proud of me.

Jeffrey Scott Weisman

GOOD DEEDS

Helped a bunch of people get out of jams.

Held the door open for nearly every woman I could.

Gave quite a few homeless people a buck or two.

Thanked just about every person I needed to.

Drove my ex's mom to the WC Memorial Hospital in Branford twice a week for over six months so that she could get her cancer treatments. And I didn't even gripe about it.

Put a skunk down that was half flattened
by a garbage truck in front of my house.

Kept my lip shut about nearly everything
I should have.

Tried to do right by people, at least most
of the time.

Never spat on my ma and pa's graves.

And those are just a few of my good
deeds.

BAD RAPS

Big Louie says he got a bad rap. That he was framed by some hustler on his home turf for working him over on a two-bit deal one night when he let his guard down. That it's all, "Just a case of mistaken identity," and "wrongful timing," and that he's, "innocent as a baby lamb."

Yeah, that's what he says.

But even Cotter and High Jinks know better than that.

CLEAN TIME

For the last few years at least, I've done nothing but keep my shit on the right side of proper. No fights, no back lip, no questionable behavior, just doing things right so that I can have a chance to get paroled while I still have some life in me. "Playing the arrow straight," Cotton likes to say, when he sees me keeping to myself in the yard. "Working the clean time," Lemme always laughs.

Damn right I am.

Jeffrey Scott Weisman

FISH

The fish start out all glory-eyed hopeful and upbeat bullish positive thinking that everything will come up roses for them if they just work at it hard enough.

Yeah, they sure do.

And Cotton thinks that's the damn near funniest thing he's ever seen too. "Look at them," he will say, as a new troop of inmates tromps in from the buses, their heads held high, smiles cracked on their lips, kicks in their steps, glimmers in their peeps, gleams on their mugs, believing that they will change the world. "Like it's them we've been waiting for."

Course, it don't take too long for that to die. Not at all.

Jeffrey Scott Weisman

JUDGED PROPER

Now sure, I'd love to be able to say that I didn't know what I was getting into or that I didn't have any other options or that I had to do what I did in order to survive or that like Lemme "I was forced into a life of crime," but that wouldn't be true, cause I knew what I was getting into before I even got started. Damn right I did.

And don't ever think otherwise.

A THEORY OF EVERYTHING

There is no past. There is no present. There is no future. There's only this infinite, eternal now. "It's all just one big sameness," I'll say to High Jinks and Cotton, plunked down in my seat, my fork in my claw, stabbing at my chow in the mess hall, nearly every chance I get. "The endless big now."

Yeah, that's my theory. My theory of everything.

PAR FOR THE COURSE

This 211 crew leader, B-Boy, has it out for me now because I wouldn't cede my spot in the yard to one of his goons the other afternoon.

And Menace is pissed at me again because I broke up a scuffle between him and Cotton the other morning outside the mess hall. "Gonna shank your ass," he said to me as I held him back, the stink of his breath slapping me in the face. "You can count on it."

And this old-timer named Rico's got something against me according to High Jinks, even though I couldn't tell you what or why. "He's madder than a bull in heat at you," High Jinks snickered, standing next to me for morning head count the other day. "And that's being kind."

And those are the only ones I know about.

Jeffrey Scott Weisman

CORPOREAL REALITIES

My face is wearing its wrinkles like an old porch. And the bulge of my nose seems to be growing into the shape of a chrysanthemum. And my thin brown hair is turning into the silver-grey hue of a saddle horse. And my dark green eyes are starting to sink into my skull like a lost treasure. And the loose skin under my chin's turning into the texture of a burlap sack. And my elongated ears and nostrils are sprouting hairs like an overgrown hayfield. And my chipped teeth have become the stained yellow color of stale coffee. And my bulbous lips are all cracked and craggy like a sunbaked strip of pavement. And the small mole on my right cheek has weathered into the texture of a rotten mushroom.

And that's only the most obvious things I see from a quick scan in the shower room mirror.

Fucking forty-nine.

Jeffrey Scott Weisman

A CHIP OFF THE OLD BLOCK

Coming up my ma used to tell me that I was no good and that I wouldn't amount to anything, that, to quote her directly, "I was nothing but a waste of good semen," and that she was, "Damn right sorry I was ever born."

Course, it takes one to know one.

A CODE OF HONOR

It should be that your word's your bond,
that your heart's your point, that your
care's your purpose, that your
sympathy's your intention, that your
sacrifice's your goal, that your help's
your aim, that your love's your drive,
that your compassion's your name.

Yeah, that's what it should be.

Jeffrey Scott Weisman

SOME WISDOM

Cotton told me this a few years back when I first ran into trouble with Menace: "You can take the fool out of the crazy, but you can't take the crazy out of the fool."

And High Jinks once said this to me while we were waiting in line for block count: "Any man can cum, but only a real man can stay."

And Big Louie cracked this out one morning while we were sitting in the mess hall: "Just cause you got eyes don't mean you can see."

And Little Crow always likes to say: "You feel with your heart, not with your head."

Now ain't that some wisdom.

Jeffrey Scott Weisman

EYES OUT

Lemme says it's the bull guards you've got to watch out for, what with their prowling block scans and random house checks and those peeps like mirrors scouring constant through the cracks. And they are something for sure, worse than the police. Got to give him that.

And Barbwire puts his weight on the other cons. He says they're the real concern around here since they don't take a day off. Or a moment. And he's got a point about that too. Cause there ain't no hiding from them, especially since they all seem to think it's just some game that will come up even for them on tax day.

But still, we all know it's the warden that you've really got to watch out for, what with those eyes that don't have to be looking at you to see what's going on. That's the real worry. Cause he's seemingly watching you even when he's not.

Hell, there ain't no dodging that.

Jeffrey Scott Weisman

SOUND ADVICE

Don't expect anyone to do anything for you.

Don't count on anyone for anything.

Anticipate the worst.

Figure it will all go wrong.

Make do with what you have.

Trust no one.

Rely on yourself.

Fight for everything.

Now, that's some sound advice.

RULES

They say we can't bark after lights out, that we can't run numbers, that we can't etch ink, that we can't trade stores, that we can't swap chow, that we can't goof candy, that we can't hold our blocks, that we can't throw down, that we can't sell wares, that we can't work the bull guards, that we can't challenge the warden, that we can't upset the order.

Yeah, that's what they say.

But we all know rules are meant to be broken.

FOR THE RECORD

My sister once told me that this boy named Randy who lived a few streets over from us when I was coming up was trying to touch her on the bus ride home from school one day. "He was doing what?" I remember saying, sitting on our couch next to her after my school let out, our old TV chattering away in front of us. "He was trying to touch me," she had answered, tears welling in her eyes. "I told him to stop." "Randy?" I simply said, looking at her.

"Yes."

So, I went over to his house, called him outside, and beat the shit out of him, telling him, "If you so much as look at her ever again, I will kill your ass."

And I felt good about that. Righteous.

That has to be said.

Jeffrey Scott Weisman

MONKEY MOUTHS

The monkey mouths just yak relentless about nothing at all. "The warden's got to change up the block walls," one of them'll froth wild, while tromping out to the yard. Or, "Those fish sitting at that table over there," another one'll rail away while shoveling chow into his piehole. "Need to find a new squat."

Rafael's one, for example, cause he'll say, "The bull guards are turning the showers into lighthouses." Like that means anything to anyone.

How fucking worthless.

MOTHER UNIVERSE

Little Crow says that the night sky is really the face of a woman, "Mother Universe," as he calls it. And that the stars are the freckles on her cheeks. And that the comets and meteors are the tears she sheds when she sees how we treat each other. "Got to care about your brothers and sisters," he likes to say, "Cause your mother is always watching you."

And I like that. Although I can't say that I believe a lick of it.

Jeffrey Scott Weisman

GOING DUTCH

The other day I thought about going dutch. And it came out of nowhere too. I was just sitting here in my bunk near lights out, scribbling in my notebook, minding my own, when I just wanted to tap out. The bark of the other dogs on the deck just too much to bear, the weight of my time just too much to hold, the struggle of the hour just too much to take, the thought of my deeds just too much to carry, the threat of Menace and B-Boy just too much to contain, figuring I could tie up my sheet and hang from the bars like a pig in a slaughterhouse.

And it didn't even scare me. Fuck.

CHOW

We get hot grits and canned eggs and boxed cereal and wheat bread and oatmeal and fruit cups and margarine and gravy biscuits and skim milk and coffee and beef tacos and chicken patties and fish sandwiches and hamburgers and meatloaf and baked potatoes and macaroni salad and black beans and tater tots and vegetable soup and canned corn and powdered juice and roast beef and meatballs and taco salad and salisbury steak and chicken fajitas and baked fish and chicken fried rice and tuna salad and cheese pizza and hot dogs and chili and pasta and coleslaw and mashed potatoes and french fries and green beans and beets and peas and cornbread and garden salad and carrots.

Jeffrey Scott Weisman

Yeah, that's what we get. And we're lucky
for that too. I know.

LESSONS LEARNED

You don't tell people how you feel.

You don't show weakness.

You don't cry.

You don't cede ground.

You don't apologize.

You don't regret.

You don't make confessions.

You don't care.

You don't get close to anyone.

Jeffrey Scott Weisman

And those are just some of the lessons
I've learned in my life.

A BOLD-FACED LIER

I remember sitting at the kitchen table with my ex one evening not long after her mom had started her chemo treatments at the WC Memorial in Branford, my ex's shoulders slumped over, her mug drooping heavy with sadness, saying, "I'm scared, babe. She doesn't look good. The treatments don't seem to be helping. She's so tired. She's hurting a lot. I don't know what I'll do without her."

"Don't worry," I replied, without a moment's hesitation, leaning forward in my seat. "She'll be alright. She's a fighter."

And I still don't know why I said that. And with such conviction too.

Jeffrey Scott Weisman

BEYOND UNDENIABLE

Some fools spend their whole lives in here fighting everything and everyone. They roar at the bull guards. They wail at the block bosses. They rage at the warden. They bawl at the yard dogs. They seethe at their bars. They cover their houses with their feces. They flood the blocks with their urine. They shank their own mugs. They chop off their own testicles. All to prove that they can't be constrained.

But some of them need to be caged. That's simply beyond undeniable.

SOME DAYS

It's one step. And then another. And then another. And then another. And then another. And then another still.

That's all I can do some days.

That's all.

One step. And then another. And then another. And then another. And then another. And then another still.

PAST LIVES

A son and brother, I'd say, that was the first. Course, I'm still that to my sister. But she wouldn't own that. "Ex-communicated," she'd say. "Cut from my blood."

A school boy would be the next, I imagine, cause I tried to make that work for a few years when I was a pup in junior high, applying myself to my studies and reading away at my books, thinking that maybe I could be one for the academy someday. But that was only temporary cause I wasn't made for that kind of life. Just not my thing.

A truant would be another, cause I spent most of my youth running around wild on the streets, getting into scrapes, looking for trouble, evading the police, one way or another. And I'm even kind of proud of that too.

A lover is certainly one. Carmen being my first. And Tonya after her.

A public nuisance, that has to be said. Hell, even been gaveled that way. A bunch of times too.

A husband, for about six years, that is.

A killer, twice over, so we're clear.

And those are only a few of my past lives. Damn.

Jeffrey Scott Weisman

HELL

The Sunday preachers like to howl about this fire and brimstone, this sorrow and suffering, this horror and affliction, these wails and screams, these lava pits and torture devices, this burning flesh and cracking bones, these open wounds and festering sores, this unrelenting agony and unfathomable pain.

But none of that seems to come close to the truth. Not even slightly. At least not from where I'm standing.

MARKING TIME

Sometimes I'll spend the whole day doing nothing but sitting here in my house watching the shadows creep across the walls like a ticking time bomb or wandering through the yard keeping my head down hoping against hope to stay out of trouble with the other cons or goose stepping through my routine like some soldier on the march, only to look up at the end of the day amazed that I'm fixing for sleep again, the scruff of my blanket coarse against my skin.

"Damn," I'll say sometimes, listening to the hoots and hollers cracking like thunder from down my block before lights out. "What did I do with myself all day?"

Jeffrey Scott Weisman

Course, even I know I've been up to something.

Marking time, I call it. Nothing more.

HIGH JINKS

High Jinks is always talking about how there's some great palace in the sky waiting for us when we die. "I know it," he likes to rasp through his cracked lips and scabbed skin that make him look like broken glass peeking out from under rotten leaves clumped behind a shed. "Because I see it when I got things configured just right."

Take that day when we were sitting in the mess hall for example when he said, "It's a guarantee," to Lemme and me chowing down on our slop with him. "No need to doubt it for a minute."

"Sure," Lemme slapped back, staring at him from across the table, Lemme's knife

43

perched in his claw like a crutch. "Money back."

"That's right," High Jinks sniggered at him through blackened gums. "You ain't got nothing to worry about."

Course, we don't call him High Jinks for nothing.

STINKS

There's stale piss and fresh shit and dripping sweat and rotten breath and nose snot and ear wax and dried semen and hair gel and cheap deodorant and passed gas and spray cologne and bar soap and medicinal shampoo and crusty scabs and canker sores and decaying gums and decomposing teeth and foot fungus and unwashed jumpers and soiled underwear and old socks and dirty shoes and chewed fingernails and flaky skin and open wounds and raw sewage and spray disinfectants and bottled cleaners and spoiled food and unflushed toilets and shower mold.

And those are just some of the stinks in here.

Jeffrey Scott Weisman

RUNNING THE SHOW

The gang bosses like to think they're running the show. That they've got their right to hold on to how things go. We see them tromping the block and pacing the yard, all puffed out proud like some plumed out peacocks trying to flaunt their wares. It's funny too. The way they've convinced themselves to that place in line, like it's some birthright calling to clutch that they've got.

Cotton likes to chuckle about that one too. "Look at them," he'll say, leaning back against the fence in the yard while they stomp around, grins on their mugs, hollering away at everyone and everything they can. "Thinking they're holding down the fort."

It's funny too because we all know who's really running the show.

And I mean all.

Jeffrey Scott Weisman

BEAT DOWN

When I was around twelve and a half, I came home from my friend Trevor's house one day and caught my pa beating the crap out of my ma in the kitchen, this can of chicken soup in his right hand, his mug strained in wrath, smacking her silly on the side of the head, blood dripping down her face, her stringy hair stained red, my ma looking up at my pa like fear in a smock.

And I didn't know what to do.

So I ran outside, praying that they didn't see me, knowing that my pa would kill me if he caught me watching them, while hoping against hope to forget the sound of that can cracking into her skull.

Damn, talk about a beat down.

CHAIN DOGS

Jasper and Snap Back don't go anywhere without each other. And by anywhere, I mean anywhere. To the crapper, there's Jasper with Snap Back. To the mess hall, there's Jasper with Snap Back. To the yard, there's Jasper with Snap Back. To the commissary, there's Jasper with Snap Back. To the shower room, there's Jasper with Snap Back.

And it's funny how so many of the other cons get all bent out of shape and riled up raw over how they tag around together like that too.

Now sure, it's true that they are chained together at the collar like some crazy-ass co-joined twins or something. But still, good for them.

That's what we should all say. Nothing more.

Jeffrey Scott Weisman

BIG PLANS

Cotter's always talking about these big plans he's got for when he gets out of here. How he's gonna set up this little shop to fix appliances and whatnot in his hood and how he's gonna find some woman and settle down and how they're gonna have a bunch of kids together, some "whole row-kicking brood and wild bunch crew", as he likes to say, and how he's gonna do right and make sure to live by the law.

Yeah, Cotter's got some big plans for when he gets out of here. And we listen to him too.

Hell, we even pretend to believe him from time to time.

FREE BIRDS

There's the religious types who come around on Sundays and holidays and preach about how much we are loved. And there's the twelve-steppers who get all frothy-mouthed self-righteous about how they were sick once too. And there's the educator-types who want to spread the word about all of their skills. And there's the head shrinks who are hoping to chase away their own kooks. And then there's the random do-gooders who need to feel better about themselves. But that's about it. Cause we're not meant to be talked about or seen. At least not by the free birds.

You know what I mean?

Jeffrey Scott Weisman

A CLEAN SHOT

Cotton says that we're all given a clean shot. That no matter your blood, no matter your history, no matter your place, no matter your upbringing, no matter your learning, no matter your parentage, no matter your checkout date, that we're all given the same clean shot at things. That's what Cotton says anyways.

But that don't seem to be how it works. Not at all.

GHOSTS

We've all got ghosts we can't shake.

Take Cotter, for example, who once bemoaned, "That damn kid," while leaning forward on the bench in the yard, his eyes heavy with sorrow, his face cracked from strain, his voice thick with confession. "She never was supposed to be there when I went into that crib." The acknowledgment of that thought harder to bear than the gavel.

And, "I just lost my mind," High Jinks once declared, shuffling along next to me in the block line. "I'll never know why I iced him out like that." The concession of that moment more profound than his breath.

Jeffrey Scott Weisman

Or, Little Crow once simply saying, "I would do it all differently if I could do it again," before gulping down the last of his OJ in the mess hall, a grimace painted on his mug.

And course, there's that old man I shot point-blank in the face when I robbed that credit union in Livingston that I keep seeing over and over in my head.

Yeah, we've all got ghosts we can't shake.

COLORS

Everything's sliced and diced up by colors in here. The blacks with the blacks. The whites with the whites. The browns with the browns. The reds with the reds. The yellows with the yellows. Hell, the greens with the greens, for that matter. That's how it works.

Course, they don't like to talk about that out there.

Those fuckers.

Jeffrey Scott Weisman

IN PLAIN SIGHT

Barbwire loses himself in his weights,
spending all his time in the rec yard, his
body all bulk and heft, bulged like some
Olympic champion.

And Lemme, he vanishes off into the
commissary, glaring all proud and tall
over another pack of ramen or some can
of beans, his cell stash like a trophy case.

Now Cotton, he gets lost in his head,
trying to work out some kind of meaning
to things, like it all will add up if he just
puts the decimal points in the right
places.

Course High Jinks, he disappears into
the ether, his whole deal about spinning

out of orbit, "temporary as it is," to quote his bunk mumbles, "worthwhile."

And me, I like my scribbles, cause it lets me take flight for a few, soaring off into the void, if I'm lucky, that is.

Yeah, seems we're all hiding in plain sight.

Jeffrey Scott Weisman

A BEST STAB

Tonya, my second girlfriend, once came home from her job at the Daneville Diner and Roadhouse feeling all sad and blue about life cause she was being treated like trash by the customers there, saying specific, "Dogs are given more compassion when they're put down. It's like they don't care about my feelings at all."

And I didn't know what to do.

So I went out to the Nichol's Gas Station near us on Eighth and bought her a dozen daises, saying, "For you babe, cause I care," when I handed them to her.

And well, that was the best I could think to do.

Jeffrey Scott Weisman

THE ALPHA MUTT

Stookie's the Alpha Mutt right now, cause he's the one who clawed and scratched, smashed and bashed, battled and clashed, brawled his way to the top of the heap like some champion prize fighter, hands metaphorically raised high, head metaphorically capped in a crown, belt metaphorically strapped around his waist, barking out orders to his underlings: "Nix that fool in the yard for me," and, "Get me my grub from the mess line," glorious like he owns the world.

Course now, it's only a matter of time before he crashes back down to Earth.

SQUIRRELS

They're all fidgety uncomfortable and anxious odd, always looking away and twitching constant about everything, like the weight of the moment's simply too much to take.

Tanner's one of them. He stands there kicking at the ground and darting his eyes all around this way and that, trying not to look you in the mug, mumbling, "Not sure, not sure," when you ask him about any old thing. What time of day is it? Or, how are you doing? For example. "Not sure, not sure." That's all he can say.

Squirrels I call them. Fucking tragic.

Jeffrey Scott Weisman

AN ANIMAL

I've had snot boogers so green-yellow and slimy huge that when I picked them out of my nose and stared at them for a minute I thought I discovered a new kind of toxic sludge.

And I've had eye goobers so crusty large and sticky stiff that when I flicked them away I was actually able to watch their trajectory soar across my bunk like a spit wad.

And I've hocked up loogies so dense gloppy and gross thick onto the yard that I could've spackled a windowpane with them.

And I've blasted a fart so juicy loud and wet warm that the track marks left on my underpants were like a roadmap to the infirmary.

And I've defecated so raunchy raw and disgusting liquid awful that I actually felt bad for the drain pipes.

And that's to say nothing of puking out my brains from time to time. Or that thing that grew on my penis once. Or that stuff that drained from my ear not too long back. Or all of the other things I could add if I dared.

Yeah, I'm an animal. But ain't we all.

Jeffrey Scott Weisman

BROODS

Cotton keeps pictures of his brood tacked above his bunk like a trophy hunter. The smirks on their mugs and the shines in their peeps beaming through those pictures something he can't get enough of.

"My boy," he likes to boast, leaning against the bars of his cell, "makes me so proud," And "my girl," he'll roar, fixing the tape on the edge of one of the pictures, "she's the apple of my eye."

And I like to listen to him too, hearing the happiness in his voice and seeing the pep in his step when he talks about his brood. "They're going to visit me as soon as they can," he'll stress, whenever he's pressed about why they don't ever stop by during visitation hours. "They're just busy, you know?"

Course, that's not why they don't see him. Even he knows that.

Jeffrey Scott Weisman

HEAD CHECK

We are counted constant around here—
at wake-up, at the showers, in the mess
hall, at work assignment, during yard
release, at education, during shift
change, during leisure time, before lights
out, to name but a few. And that's not
even including the unexpected ones like
lockdowns and shakedowns that happen
for the inevitable house raids, fights,
escape attempts, bull guard suspicions,
and all.

But still, even we don't know how many
of us there are in here. Not a clue.

SQUAWKS

Squawks think that if they just scream at you long and loud enough that you will somehow cede to what they have to say. That by raising their voice, spitting in your mug, and drowning out your response that they will win.

Squint's like that. He'll rant and rave till he's blue in the face about how you just have to see it his way. "It's fundamental," he will add when he's finally about to take a breath. "Any fool can see that."

Course, that's why they're called squawks, cause of the noise they make, not cause of the action they create.

Jeffrey Scott Weisman

GEM

There used to be this feral cat that lived under the shed at my ma and pa's house in Courville when I was coming up. And she was something else too, all mangy skinned and clumped grey hair small, with one eye that was half-closed from getting in a scrum and a back leg that was shorter than another. Genetics, I suppose. Born that way.

And that cat could yowl like no one's business. Sometimes she would just sit under that shed and cry for hours and hours on end. Course, pa, couldn't stand her. Even shot at her once. But she evaded him, no problem.

And I'd feed her table scraps from time to time too by putting them out near the shed cause I wanted to take care of her the best I could. But it was real hard cause that cat didn't want anything to do with anyone. Although I did pet her once. Even heard her purr. And that was quite a moment too. I was sitting in front of the shed whittling a stick when that cat came walking around the corner and came right up to me, letting me pet her back for a few seconds, purring away like an old lawnmower engine. "Gem," I called her then. "My Gem."

Damn I miss that cat.

Jeffrey Scott Weisman

HUSTLES

Been a gas station attendant, working the cash register and stocking the shelves, all for a few bucks a day.

And a house painter, grinding away as one of the crew, scraping siding and priming boards, only so that they could be covered right back up.

And a tractor salesman, although I wasn't very good at that. Not because I couldn't sell the con, but because I didn't care to. (And I worked that gig twice too.)

And a car thief, for a good part of my youth and early twenties, that is.

And a bank robber, for most of my adulthood, making a decent go at that, in fact. Seven plus grand on average a job, easy.

And those are only a few of the hustles that I will confess to.

Jeffrey Scott Weisman

VISITATION RIGHTS

Cotter and Barbwire live for their visitation rights. The whole month yapping away endless about how they can't wait for their wives to come see them. "Gonna kick with my babe," Cotter likes to declare. "Some one-on-one time," Barbwire will add, leaning back in his bunk, the barks from the other cons howling around us.

Now granted, neither of them talk much about love. But regardless, I'm envious.

CAPITAL P'S

Cotter's one and so is High Jinks and this yard dog named Shefford's certainly one too, cause they'll do anything and everything they have to in order to ingratiate themselves into whatever situation they're in.

For example, at the first sign of trouble, Cotter will be out in the yard, trailing along after one of the main block hounds, stammering, "Can I do something for you, my brother?" Or, "Do you need anything, boss?"

Or, High Jinks will stop by someone's house, offering to tidy up the place, merely to stay in their good graces. And that's the only reason too.

But neither of them have a thing on Shefford cause that fool will sell out his ma in order to keep on the right side of things, saying, "You couldn't be more correct," or, "Whatever you say, boss," at the drop of a hat.

Capital P's I call them. Short for pussies.

GREASED WHEELS

In here, the only way to get anything done at all is to play the scene proper. Need a new razor, scratch a back. Need a clean chow plate, scratch a back. Need a fresh jumper, scratch a back. That's how it works.

"Greased wheels," Big Louie calls it.

Bullshit myself.

Jeffrey Scott Weisman

A HARD TRUTH

When I first got into some real trouble with the law for jacking cars in my hometown when I was eighteen, the circuit court judge in Wellington County who was presiding over my case looked at me for a second from the bench, his beard white with age, his peeps gleaming with purpose, his robe pressed clean around his lanky frame, and said, "Son, I hope you know you can't outrun yourself," before gaveling me guilty.

Now ain't that some truth.

INKED UP

Lemme's got a ladybug brandishing a pill bottle. "For my mother," as he likes to say, while chuckling so violently his body nearly shakes apart. "And her endearing love."

And Cotter has two tear drops, one for each of his brothers, Erickson and Anthony, to label them proper.

And Booker has a broken heart with a knife through it. "For the death of my daughter," as he once told Cotton while we stood in line outside the mess hall waiting for the bull guards to let us in. "So that I never forget."

And Squint and Rafael are straight-up sleeved out to the max. Even tagged on their eyelids. Simply hoping against hope to keep the world from catching their peeps.

And that's only a few.

Course, we're all inked up. Whether you can see them or not.

FEALTY AND WHATNOT

We wear our allegiances like shields around here. Nearly all of us calling some crew or gang their own.

"It's how you survive," Barbwire likes to stress, flashing his signs and donning his ink, proud like a patriot, while we work out in the rec area.

"Gotta have a tribe," Big Louie will growl, his fangs glimmering in the afternoon sun, while lumbering across the yard. "It's madness otherwise."

Course, that loyalty don't run blood deep. No matter what anyone says.

Jeffrey Scott Weisman

THE BIG HOUSE

Cotton says that the reason we want to blow up our big house is because we can't stand it. And that sure makes sense. But Little Crow disagrees. "It's that we don't want to believe it's our home," he says, confusing us all. But Lemme's got his own take entirely. To him, "it's because we don't want it to think about it," as he likes to stress.

Course, I'm not sure about any of that.

But I do know that we're all aiming to blow it up. Whether we want to admit it or not.

SCARS

Got an old gash on my forehead from that time I crashed on my skateboard when I was fourteen while I was racing my buddy Trevor down Taylor Street in Branford.

Got a pretty gnarly cut on my lower back from when my grandma accidentally dropped me into the kitchen sink in her double-wide in Livingston when I was two.

Got an old puncture wound on my right side from that day this fish shanked me a few years back because he thought I was this con named Leroy.

Jeffrey Scott Weisman

Got a jagged stitch line on my right thigh from that night I got hung up on this wire fence outside Bakerville while I was trying to ditch the police.

Got a mangled finger from when I smashed it between two steel plates while I was working in the machine shop.

And that's only to name a few.

Course, it's the ones you don't see that hurt the most.

ROOSTERS

Otto thinks that he rules the roost. That the sun rises when he says so. That the bull guards exist for his every command. That the yard dogs move at his behest. That time itself unfolds because he says so.

And it's something else too. The way he'll strut around the yard, head held high, chest puffed out, arms flapping at his side, pecking at the turf like some cock in a coop. "Look at that fool," Lemme will say when Otto's clucking crazy about something or other going on in the yard. "Thinking he rules the roost."

Yeah, Otto's funny like that.

But he's only one of the multitude. And
that's being too kind.

THE NATURE OF THINGS

Lemme told me that his momma once said, "You ain't no good, boy," while he was perched over her knee in the kitchen, her wooden spatula in her hand, her day dress twisted around her neck, whacking him repeated like some wild dog.

"But I can't help it, momma," he had cried back between whacks, his bare skin burning sore from the beating. "It's what you taught me."

"That's right," she answered him, thumping down on him again, the crack of her spatula smacking in his ears. "You ain't no good, boy."

Jeffrey Scott Weisman

Talk about a lesson.

CALL IT KARMA

Years back, I stole this GT bicycle from outside the Kroger store in Branford, and while my friend Trevor and I were in the County Market near his house later that afternoon buying something to drink, someone stole my bicycle from outside that store, just snatched it right out from under me.

"Where'd your bike go?" I remember Trevor asking me, standing outside the County Market with his cherry pop in his hand, when we realized it was gone. "Your bike was right here."

"I know," I answered, looking up and down Stockton Street. "That was mine."

Jeffrey Scott Weisman

And I still don't know what to make of
that.

WILDFIRE

In here, we hang onto gossip like it's some kind of necessity, thinking that it's gonna matter in the big swing of things. Like the dirt on Cotter or High Jinks or even one of the bull guards, for that matter, is gonna make a difference somehow.

Take that time when we all got wind that one of the prison counselors, this young broad with shoulder-length brown hair and makeup pasted-on thick like molasses, got caught in this triste with one of the bull guards watching over the infirmary. Hell, you would've thought that the whole place had lost its mind. High Jinks saying, "I hear they're paying off the warden to steal that time." And Cotton yammering back, "Nah man, he's in on the gig."

Course, a week or so later no one even remembered a thing about it. But it sure was all the rage for that week or so there. Like wildfire, in fact.

But really, that's no different than anywhere else.

PRAYERS

Some of us pray to God. And some of us pray for the ability to do good. And some of us pray for our families. And some of us pray for the sick. And some of us pray for the lost. And some of us pray for ourselves. And some of us pray for each other. And some of us pray for our fears.

But no matter, cause we're all praying to hold on.

Jeffrey Scott Weisman

THE WEIGHT OF THINGS

When my daughter Eva died in my ex's womb from some heart condition that we couldn't do nothing about, dying before she even had a chance to live.

When my grandpa Arnold passed before I could tell him how much he meant to me.

When I told my ex, "It was your fault" after Eva died. Even though I knew it wasn't.

When I heard my old girlfriend Carmen say, "I can't be with you anymore," not long after we moved in together.

When I stopped caring about anything.

When I saw the look in that old man's eyes when I shot him point-blank in the mug.

When I begged God to forgive me.

And those are just a few that come to mind.

Jeffrey Scott Weisman

OUR HOODS

Our hoods (AKA our blocks) are coded in status around here. We've got our first-rate hoods. And our prime-time hoods. And our no-style hoods. And our down-and-out hoods. And our loon-time hoods. And reject hoods. And the hoods that no one can stand.

But really, that's the same everywhere you go.

At least that's what I say.

RETIREMENT

Cotter calls it your "sentence termination." And Lemme your "institutional let go." And High Jinks simply "paroled." And Big Louie "retirement." But regardless, they all mean the same thing—your release date.

It's just too bad that so few of us know how to handle it.

Retirement, that is.

Jeffrey Scott Weisman

ONE FOR THE TEAM

To say, when I did go to high school, I'd usually end up spending most of my time in detention hall. So much so, in fact, that this teacher, Mr. Bradwell, who ran the hall, once asked me to explain to him why I insisted on getting into trouble all of the time. "What's my justification for doing wrong?" as he so eloquently put it.

And while I thought it was an absurd thing to ask me, I did think about it for a minute before answering him that my justification for doing wrong is that there isn't any point in doing right. And my proof for that is that evil wins and that bad triumphs and that crime pays and that suffering is the norm. So rather than fight it, join it. That's what I said.

And no, he didn't like my answer. Not at all.

Jeffrey Scott Weisman

SHEEPLE

They do whatever someone says. "Get in line now," some block boss will bark, and they will instantly line up like chicks to a hen. Or, "Put those trays away," a mess hall supervisor will crack, and they will race to the bin to add their tray to the pile like fish in a call line. Or, one of the yard hounds will tell them that the searchlights are really cameras, and they will say, "I know, I know," so fast that your head will spin simply trying to see where that insanity was coming from.

Really, it's sickening.

BUGS

Bugs are everywhere. They're in the corners of the blocks. They're in the walls of the yard. They're in the doors of the mess hall. They're in the drains of the showers. They're in the cracks of the mailroom. They're in the desks of the classrooms. They're in the gates of the commissary. They're in the vents of the heating system. Hell, they're in the bunk above you, for that matter. Now sure, in here, they're what we call the prison staff who you can't trust. But really, they're anyone that exists like that.

Bugs, we call them. Fucking vermin.

Jeffrey Scott Weisman

TALL TALES

Lemme says he once stole fifty cars in a single night. And Cotton boasts about sleeping with a thousand women. And Big Louie brags about playing some uptown man for a hundred grand. And High Jinks likes to spin about, "Spending three weeks in Mexico cozying up to every drug lord in the country." And Cotter about "icing out half his town." And I'll even rip out my yarn from time to time about putting a man in the hospital once for peeping at some woman in the Littleton Bar the wrong way.

Tall tales, you know. We all spill them.

TURNING ON A MOMENT

One second, you're just walking down Finley Street, the car tires humming in your ears, the Courville city lights glaring in your peeps, the Hooper Lounge gin spinning in your head, minding your own, thinking about how you've got to get your life together, how you need to find a real job, how you've been mixed up with things you don't mean to be ever since you got out of prison, how you've been running with the wrong crowd again, how you know you're better than that, when some guy jumps out from the alleyway on your right, rags dangling from his bones, brandishing some knife at your mug, while barking about how you, "Better give me every damn penny you've got buddy."

And the next second you're stealing the knife away from him and jabbing him in the gut with it ten times, not even thinking about what you're doing, just trying to stay alive, before fleeing off down Finley Street, the taste of madness in your mouth, rage running through your veins, fear plaguing your mind.

Damn, it's crazy how everything turns on a moment.

Just crazy.

BARGAINS

Big Louie likes to sit back in his bunk, his head propped against the cinder blocks, his legs drooped over the side of his mattress, blathering stupid about how he got, "Two packs of cigs for the price of one," off Lemme. Or how he scored, "A case of soup for some weak Pruno," while working in the mess hall.

And Cotter will prattle away endlessly about how he traded a few months in the seg for his name in the yard. "Worth it ten times over," he will say any chance he gets.

And High Jinks will babble for hours on end about how he sold his life for a few hours of flight time. "Bargaining fair," to quote him directly.

And Barbwire will squeal worse than a barnyard sow in heat that it was worth every second of his sentence to have iced out that judge.

But still, I can't say any of those are real bargains. If you know what I mean.

PROJECTORS

Barbwire's one. Hell, he gets all angry-eyed riled, glaring irate peeved at everyone and everything, thinking that what he says others are doing isn't what he's doing himself. And he's clueless about that too. "Don't go cheating on my hand," he'll chime in, while working to scam you raw at a game of spades. Or, "Keep your fairy tales to yourself," he'll reply, while spewing falsities in your face like a carnie barker.

And it's a crime too. The way he projects himself onto everyone like that.

Jeffrey Scott Weisman

EINSTEIN

There used to be this con in here named Johnson who was the smartest fool I ever met. He could tell you the name of every capital in the country. And every chemical on the periodic table. And every key battle in history. And every major law there was. And that's just to scratch the surface.

"Look at Einstein there," Little Crow used to say, pointing at him sitting in the yard, Johnson's knees folded underneath him, his back pressed against the wall, reading every book in the library here. "Trying to learn the world."

Course, none of that did him a damn bit of good when this fool Kato shanked him one afternoon in order to earn his rank. But we don't like to talk about that. Not a one of us.

Jeffrey Scott Weisman

LOOSE LIPS

Back in my early twenties, I was in with this crew that jacked cars from the auto dealerships in our area and sold them to this chop shop a few towns over from us, made a decent payday at it too. A couple hundred a night easy. And that was for each of us.

"Easy squeezy," our ringleader Shaquin liked to whoop, stashing the cash in his pockets, just to make it clear.

Course, that didn't last long, cause one of the guys in our crew, this newbie named Benson, chirped silly to the cops when he was busted buying an engagement ring with marked money for his girlfriend at the Spanner Pawn Shop in Littleton from this sting operation they were working on us.

Fucking tool.

Jeffrey Scott Weisman

PEN PALS

There's these women some of us know in here who glom onto us like shit to a shoe. Writing about how they love us and how they want to help us and how they need us and how they'll do anything for us and how we're just misunderstood and need to be saved and cared for and loved and then we will be good.

It's sad if you think about it. Truly, truly sad.

NIGHT TERRORS

Cotton says that the reason people scream like they do around here in the night is because they can't stand their time in the day. "It's their hours that get to them," he once said, while shuffling in the block line at wake-up, the other cons all scratching at their mugs or tugging at their jumpers beside me. And while that might be true, it don't seem to dig down deep enough to me, cause those screams are just too terror filled and horror loud primal to merely be about the pain of their time.

See myself, I think the reason people scream like they do in the night around here is because they can't stand who they are in the day.

Jeffrey Scott Weisman

That's what I think at least.

CLUELESS

That my grandpa had cancer.

That my ex was having an affair.

That the cops were onto me about my bank robbing scheme for nearly a year before they nabbed me that first time.

That my ma and pa were not married.

That my sister had a miscarriage when she was in high school.

That this old cellie of mine named Prax was really a rat working for the bull guards.

Jeffrey Scott Weisman

That my gym teacher in junior high, Mr. Elroy, was molesting half of the boys in the school locker room.

That my first parole officer was actually connected to the mob.

Yeah, it's crazy how fucking clueless I can be.

STRAIGHT PERPLEXED

The other afternoon I saw a Rico's head get bashed in so badly that his brains were literally oozing out through his ear holes. Just green and yellow mush squished out on the concrete worse than some possum run over on the highway.

It was fucking disgusting.

And next to Rico's head in the yard was a dandelion growing up though a crack in the concrete. The dandelion looking all gentle and alive straining for a ray of sunshine.

And I didn't know what to make of that. I really, really didn't.

Jeffrey Scott Weisman

Although, to say, that at least solved one
of my problems for me.

THE COMPOUND

We've got a commissary and a hospital and a rec yard and a movie theater and a chapel and some bunk houses and classrooms and work centers and hood blocks and administrative buildings and maintenance sheds and crosswalks and parking lots and roadways, to name but a few.

Our city, that is, the compound. What we call our home.

Jeffrey Scott Weisman

PRICELESS

I remember this night not too long after I first met my ex when I was lying naked with her in bed in her basement apartment in Lincolnshire, her body against mine, her face resting against my chest, my hand caressing her shoulder, revealing my hopes to her about our future together. "I want a family too," she had said after hearing me tell her how I wanted to have children with her someday, the conviction in her voice unforgettable.

"I'm glad," I replied, sincerely grateful for having her in my life. "Blessed."

Damn, I wish I could go back there.

MENACE

Menace collects notches like most people collect tats, simply carving out numbers on his belt like an undertaker. And he's all proud of that too, barking out, "Don't go thinking I won't ice you out over some chow," while he's being carted away by the bull guards after pulling off another shanking, or, "Don't dare glance at me wrong fools," while he's being tased in the yard for trying to take out another fish.

And he's crazy like that too. "Consciousless," Jasper once said. "Not even a hint of remorse," Lemme piled on. Scary as shit, I'd say (especially since I'm on his mark right now).

Jeffrey Scott Weisman

But at least he's tagged proper.

BARKERS

There's fools in here who bark about women like other men breathe. Just staring at some clipping they've got posted on their house wall for hours on end, yelping constant about everything they'd do to her if they could, howling endless about every conquest they've ever had.

"I'd tear her in half," one of them'll say, a dribble of salvia curling at his mouth when we catch of a glimpse of a female bull guard in the chow line. "And make her beg for more."

"She wouldn't even be able to walk again," another one'll return, his tongue hanging over his lower lip like a mutt in estrus.

And yeah, I get the draw, but not the bark.

SOLITARY CONFINEMENT

Technically it's called the segregation unit in here, that's the place they throw you when they want to separate you from everyone else. The hole, in common parlance, that is. And it's rough too, cause it's so lonely and cold, desolate and isolated, detached and despondent, dispirited and crestfallen, woebegone and depressed.

But the truth is, no one has to put you in the segregation unit in order for you to be in solitary confinement. Cause that's not how it works.

Torturous as that is.

Jeffrey Scott Weisman

COYOTES

Cotton's one. And so is Booker. And my old childhood buddy Trevor was one too. Cause they're all the same. They run with themselves. They keep to their own. They listen to their own rhythms. They follow their own ways.

"Coyotes," Little Crow calls them.

Genuine, I'd add. For real.

NOT FUNNY

Lemme thinks the story of how I was once busted driving this girl I liked, Tricia Martin, to her cosmetics class in Littleton is the funniest story he ever heard. Course, I don't.

See, I had stolen this Camaro the night before from this mechanic's shop in Bakerville, and I hadn't had a chance to dump it off yet, so I had just left it parked in the carport behind my apartment I was renting with my buddy Trevor at the time, and Tricia came by my place, noticed the car, and asked me to drive her to school. "Come on, please," she had said, when I initially resisted. "My truck's broke. I need a ride." "Fine," I finally relented, not knowing what else I could do. I didn't want her to know that I was jacking cars for a living.

So, I drove her to school, making sure to keep on my best behavior, when I was pulled over in Littleton for seemingly no reason at all. "What'd I do?" I asked the cop when he ordered me out of the car. "I wasn't speeding or anything." "That's my car," the cop simply answered, throwing me up against his hood, the click of his cuffs clacking in my ears, my arms pressed around my back. "It was stolen last night from the Quality Auto Shop in Bakerville."

And no I didn't have a response to that. Not at all.

SCRIBBLES

A teacher in here told me a little while back that I should start scribbling down what I'm thinking, telling me specific, "If you get it out of you and look at it, you can see what it really is you're dealing with. You can see who you really are."

And I liked that advice.

Course, I can't say it's helped me none. I really can't.

But anything's worth a shot.

Jeffrey Scott Weisman

DEMONS

I see these messed-up faces in my sleep,
wailing away at me in pain, the howls of
their suffering like an inexplicable horror
show.

I see my ma and pa laughing at me while
they lock me in my room so that they can
go on a drug run.

I see Tricia Martin snickering at me cause
I couldn't get it up after drinking all night.

I see my fourth grade teacher, Mr.
Randolph, calling me worthless cause I
didn't have a lunch to bring to school.

I see the face of that old man I shot point-
blank looking so scared at me.

I see my sister telling me I should never talk to her again.

I see my grandpa Arnold collapsing in front of me from a heart attack when I was fifteen.

And those are just a few of my demons.

Just a few.

Jeffrey Scott Weisman

DEATH ROW

The truth is, we all end up on death row. Every damn one of us. Now sure, some of us get there in better ways than others. And some of us have more time than others. And some of us might even have an easier go of it than others. But no matter, cause we're all gonna end up on death row.

One way or another. That's for sure.

SIGHTS

There's chipped paint and cracked
concrete and cinder blocks and steel
plates and iron bars and stained
plexiglass and metal benches and
grizzled maws and pockmarked mugs
and bald domes and botched tats and
scarred tissue and faded jumpers and
worn sneakers and fluorescent bulbs and
corrugated steps and dead grass and
brown turf and patched asphalt and
armed towers and rail posts and
basketball rims and wire fences and light
poles and guard badges and slouched
backs and flabby guts and muscled
necks and mesh netting and exposed
pipes and oiled hair and clipped beards
and plastic utensils and paper napkins
and scuffed floors and dirty toilets and

133

scratched tiles and dripping faucets and locked halls and bolted doors and galvanized gates.

And those are just some of the sights in here.

SURVIVAL KITS

A sheet, a blanket, a pillowcase, two pairs of underwear, two t-shirts, a bag with one small bar of soap, one mini toothpaste, one mini pencil, a shaving razor, a cup, and a spoon.

And that's it.

Just so we're clear.

Jeffrey Scott Weisman

SINS

I once snatched a peep of my sister changing in her bedroom, her flabby breasts flopping across her chest, the tips of her nipples glistening under the lights, and I couldn't stop staring.

I coveted quite a few women while I was married to my ex, one only a few hours after we got hitched, for some damn reason.

I've stolen everything I could get my hands on, including cars and trucks and vans and SUVs and all the money I could. And yeah, I should probably stop there.

I've lied at will.

I've murdered two men.

I've wished for forgiveness.

I've failed, repeatedly.

And those are only a few of my sins that
I can recall right now.

Jeffrey Scott Weisman

FLESH AND BONE

Sometimes I wonder if I'm more than just this flesh and bone that I'm squatting in. That, in fact, I'm really this soul that the Sunday preachers like to talk about. And that that is the real me.

Yeah, sometimes I wonder about that.

But only sometimes.

POETRY

A year or so back, I watched this fish walk up to this old timer sitting at a table in the mess hall with a few other cons, smack him across the mug with his chow tray two times, bark at him, "Don't ever fucking look at me like that again," and then stand there and wait for the bull guards to haul him away. The old timer simply sitting there holding his claw to his face, a welt the size of a baseball popping off on his cheek.

Now talk about some poetry. Damn.

A MASTER PLAN

There was this kid I knew when I was coming up named Traylon. And he was something else too. Real kind and smart, funny and caring, personable and generous. Hell, everyone liked him. "That kid's going somewhere," my old running mate Trevor would say when we would see him loping down the street. "There's no doubt about that." And I agreed with him too.

And then one day our high school principal, Mr. Conway, told us that he was killed by some truck driver who fell asleep at the wheel while he was waiting to cross the intersection at Randolph and Seventh near his house. Simply iced out in a second.

And I didn't know what to make of that.

Course, everyone kept telling me that it happened for some divine purpose and that it was part of some master plan. But I really don't see how that could be true.

Not at all.

Jeffrey Scott Weisman

HARD TIME

Don't think it's the madness that kills you.
Or the regs. Or the shanks. Or the
squabbles. Or the yard dogs. Or the
block bosses. Or the bull guards. Or the
dying even, for that matter.

It's the living that does. We all know that.

AN OAK TREE

There's this giant oak tree in the field behind the wall on the east side of the prison that must be at least a hundred years old. The trunk on it as thick as a truck, the branches on it as broad as a shed, the leaves on it as abundant as a corn field, the whole thing sitting there like some ancient Buddha, perched under the sun.

And that tree was there long before I was. And it will be there long after I am gone. And it doesn't care a wit about either of those things.

Damn, I wish that I could say that about me.

Jeffrey Scott Weisman

SCARED SHITLESS

The first time I stepped into a prison was after I caught my ten month case for running with that carjacking ring when I was twenty-two years old.

And I remember it like it was yesterday too, getting off the bus, the bull guards scowling all over the place, the other inmates looking around all cockeyed at everything, the cons in the yard staring over at us like we were fresh bait, this head boss barking orders at us to, "Get your carcasses into line," while we tromped down the bus stairs, the shine of the sun stinging my eyes, the look of the iron gates and the concrete walls and the wire fences and the watch towers and the searchlights looming around me like something more real than reality itself, while the cons in the yard hooted and leered in joy.

Course, I acted like I wasn't scared.

Damn right I did.

Jeffrey Scott Weisman

NO JOKE

"Storms," Lemme likes to call them. And that's about right too. Cause they're what happens when your house gets torn apart, when your stuff gets strewn asunder, when your personal rig gets trashed, when your whole place gets wrecked to all hell and back by the bull guards searching crazy for whatever it is they're after. The threat of one of their raids looming over you constant.

And it takes weeks after one of their shakedowns just to get the basics of your house back in order. And that's if you're lucky.

Course, we mean something different in here when we talk about storms than what people on the outside do. But whether they're natural or not, they both destroy your place stupid.

And that ain't no joke.

Jeffrey Scott Weisman

FEARS

That my health will fail me.

That I'll fuck up again.

That I'll die in here.

That I'll die alone.

That I won't be able to avoid Menace.

That I can't make it on the outside.

That I'm irredeemable.

That I'm destined to be a failure.

Yeah, those are certainly a few of my fears.

BRAKE FLUID

At least half the cons are on brake fluid around here. And that's being generous. Cause most are taking something for anxiety and for stress and for depression and for bipolar disorder and for schizophrenia or for whatever else you can think of.

Course, that ain't no different than anywhere else. That's got to be said.

Jeffrey Scott Weisman

LONE SHARKS

In here, we operate under the rule of the loan sharks—get two today for ten back tomorrow. And it's a real crime too. The way those loan sharks hold out their paws, turn up their mugs, glare at you through their peeps, while doling out their goods like dime-store candy. The whole time knowing that they've got you worse than a city banker.

Cheddar's one of them. You'll see him out in the yard, standing next to some yard dog, the yard dog desperate for some phone money or commissary goods or Pruno or whatnot, taking whatever terms he can get. Chedder so content with his position that he'll openly joke about his status. "Living it up like the rich and famous," he'll snicker, clenching onto his wad of notes. "Anything I want."

And he's just one of that ilk too. That's for sure.

Jeffrey Scott Weisman

SPEECHLESS

My grandpa Arnold used to listen to me tell him about how I wanted to be a professional baseball player when I grew up. How I wanted to play shortstop and be the leadoff man cause that way I could manage the infield and set the tone for my team. How I wanted to make enough money to move him and my grandma out of their trailer in Livingston. And how I wanted to help other kids like me do something with their lives.

"I believe in you," he would say, sitting in his recliner on the front porch, a plug of tobacco in his maw, a glass of whiskey in his hand. "You might not be able to do everything you want in life, but you'll be able to do some of the things you want in life. That's for sure. And don't ever forget that. I believe in you. Damn right I do."

God that meant everything to me. More than words can convey.

Jeffrey Scott Weisman

THE VALUE OF THINGS

Cotton says it's respect. "That if we just respected each other enough, we would have it all worked out." And High Jinks says it's love. "Even if it was the kind of love that we have for a nice piece of steak," as he once groaned while we were waiting in line at the morning head count, "or for your dog, that would be enough." And Little Crow says it's compassion. "The kind of compassion that lets you understand that we all suffer," as he once put it, leaning up against the bars outside his house. "And that hardship and strife are the norm of things."

And I think all of those make sense. I really do. But if I had to decide, I would simply say it's forgiveness. "Like that whole thing Jesus preached." Cause we all fail in life.

Yeah, that would be enough. Even if I can't do that myself.

Jeffrey Scott Weisman

TENORS

K-Bomb got out of the hole the other day. And now, the whole place is on edge. All the cons in the yard are looking over their shoulders, the bull guards are clutching onto their tasers, hell, the warden's even glaring out his window, scanning for trouble. And they're right to do that too cause K-Bomb's like a tinderbox. "He'll explode faster than a wet log on a bonfire," Barbwire likes to say, watching him haul his chow tray around the mess hall. "Worse than Menace."

It's nuts how one fool can change the whole tenor of a place. It really is.

COMING UP ACES

My pa used to say that all that mattered in life was how you died. That as long as you had your head up and your shoes on, you came out on top. That if you owed nothing to no one, left your till bone dry, and didn't have to fret about a thing, you won.

And even given the bastard that he was, that sounds about right to me.

Jeffrey Scott Weisman

POWER TRIPS

Seems like everyone's on a power trip around here. From the yard dogs playing like they own the place, to the gang bosses thinking they run the roost, to the bull guards barking out orders like they're the kings of the castle, to the warden hammering out commands like he's Christ incarnate himself, it's madness.

Course, the worst are the cowboys, the new correctional officers that is, cause they all act like they can do whatever they want to you, even though they know they can't.

Yeah, they're the worst since as the saying goes, "any kind of power corrupts anyone absolutely." Or something like that.

And ain't that true.

Jeffrey Scott Weisman

MY ANGEL

Dear Eva, I would say, I know I never got to know you. And I know I never got to hold you. And I know I never got to meet you. But I'm proud of you. You brought light into this world. You made your mom happy. You made me happy. You made everyone happy. So thank you Sweetie. You're my angel in the stars.

Yeah, that's what I would say.

DREAMS

All I want to do anymore is own a little
abode somewhere out in the country, find
me a nice woman to bed down with, take
care of her the best I can, get an old
pickup truck, a decent paying job, and do
the world right. Yeah, that's about it.

Course, we all have dreams.

Jeffrey Scott Weisman

THE MEANING OF LIFE

I'd say it comes down to either propagation or preservation since life has to make life in order for there to be life and life has to persevere so that it can exist. But if I had to pick one, I'd say it's preservation. Cause there ain't no life if you ain't alive.

Yeah, that's the real meaning of life. But I could be wrong about that.

CLOSE CALLS

There was this time when I was nine and I lost track of what I was doing and rode my bicycle right in front of this truck on Linford Street, the truck skidding to a stop in front of me, the bumper of the truck missing me by mere inches.

And then there was that day when my friend Trevor and I took his dad's rifle out behind his house and he decided to point it at me after we loaded it up, thinking it would be fun to see me shit my pants. Which I did.

And there was that night my ex and I got so drunk that I don't even remember driving home from the Lincolnshire Pub, just saw our car parked in the front yard of our apartment building the next morning, sideways no less.

And then there was that time one of my fences put a hit out on me, all over a misunderstanding about a job we did.

And then there was that fool Mason in here who shanked my ass.

Yeah, those were some of my close calls.

Just some too.

CAGED

Iron gates and concrete walls and metal bars and watch towers and barbed wires and electric fences and spotlights and house checks and door locks and bull guards and security cameras and body searches and hand tasers and gas canisters and face shields and metal batons and rubber bullets and shotguns and head counts and time checks and raid squads and whatever the hell else you can think of.

Yet still, they can't keep us totally locked down. Cause that ain't how it works. No matter where you are.

And don't ever forget that.

HOPE

A few days back Cotton told me this while we were waiting in line for head count: "Hope is like a cancer, it grows and grows until it kills you." "You think?" I replied, not sure what to make of that. "Sure do," he answered, looking back at me, the lines on his face cracked thick with age. "It's what fools do when they know they've got nothing else left."

Now damn, ain't that a bitch.

HOLIDAYS

Course, we celebrate holidays in here. We've got Thanksgiving and Christmas and New Year's, specifically, and even most religious holidays like Easter and Kwanza and Ramadan and Yom Kipper, to name a few. And we do that with a special meal, maybe a group activity of some kind or a little extra worship time in the chapel and doing whatever with your crew. But that's about it cause we're really just trying to get it over with, even if we don't want to say that out loud.

Funny though, that doesn't sound too much different than on the outside. You know what I mean?

Jeffrey Scott Weisman

PLUM USELESS

After I caught my stint for robbing that credit union in Baxter, my ex would come to visit me in prison from time to time. Until I told her to stop, that is.

And she would always come dolled up in her best pink dress too, her shoulder-length black hair always permed proper, her thin face always painted stunning, her favorite pearl necklace always on, the phone pressed against her earhole, yapping away at me from behind the plexiglass about how, "You don't need me to worry about me, babe. I can take of myself." The last time adding, "I'm doing fine without you," even.

And talk about feeling useless. Less than a man. Fuck.

Jeffrey Scott Weisman

THE BLAME GAME

Seems like everyone wants to blame someone for their life or their situation or their troubles or what-have-you. Cotter, for example, likes to say, "It's my momma's fault that I turned out like I did because she let her boyfriend molest me when I was a kid." And High Jinks will declare any chance he gets, "If my priest at my church didn't try to scare the life out of me when I was coming up, I wouldn't have this death wish now." And while they certainly have a point about that, they don't have an excuse.

Hell, none of us do. That's why it's called our life.

TITLES

Chedder goes by Block Man. And Otto, Mr. Pruno. And Jasper, Top Shelf. And the warden, Lead Boss. Any this one bull guard, Head Honcho. And this other bull guard, The Big Cheese. And this counselor, Doc Kook. And that's just to name a few.

Crazy though that anyone would think that any of that matters.

At least in the end.

Jeffrey Scott Weisman

IN A HEARTBEAT

With Eva.

With that old man.

With my ex's mom.

With Traylon from high school.

With that con Johnson.

With any sick kid.

With every dying kid.

With my younger self.

And all in a heartbeat.

No doubt.

REPLAYS

Cotton says it's the replays that get you. That's what he calls them anyways. "It's those replays playing in your head that you've got to watch out for," to quote him directly, "since they won't leave you alone." And he's got a point about that. They do bug you something serious cause you keep running over and over in your head what you wish you had done. Though some of us can hide pretty good from them. And I told Cotton that too. "Some of us just don't mind the script," that's what I said. "Cause we can change it up at will."

And he gave me that once when we were out in the yard. "Yeah, some of us do have the ability to write our own show," that's what he said. So that's got to be called fair.

Even if that's only true for some of us.

Jeffrey Scott Weisman

CELLIES

My ma and pa, my sister, my buddy Trevor (till he left the state, that is), these two goons Roger and Carl, my first girlfriend Carmen, this nutjob named Bentley, some other nutjob named Shelton, my second girlfriend Tonya, my cousin Gerome, some dude named Chris, this woman Tenisha, my ex, this con Trenton, this con Prax, this con Deion, this con Isiah, this con Malcolm, this con Tala, this con Carlos, this con Vinnie, and now Lemme.

Yeah, those have been just a few of my cellies.

At least that I can recall.

FOR US

Not long after I got out of prison for robbing that credit union in Baxter, I went up to the Kroger store in Lincolnshire, bought some quartered chicken thighs, fresh asparagus, fingerling potatoes, baked rolls, a bottle of Merlot, a Dutch apple pie, and some whipped cream and came back to our place and fixed my ex a nice dinner of fried chicken. And when we sat down to eat, the table dolled up nice, candles out, my ex looked at me and asked, "What's this for, babe?"

"Us," I proudly answered, meaning every bit of it.

Damn right I did.

Jeffrey Scott Weisman

HOTHOUSE HENS

They sneak around everywhere they go, looking to pilfer this or filch that, snatching whatever they can right out from underneath you. "Keep your eyes wide," Big Louie likes to say, whenever he sees Rafael hovering around his cell. "No shit," Lemmie will add, his peeps locked on Barbwire whenever he's around. "We've got a hothouse hen in the house."

And that's a fact. The impressiveness of their prowess aside.

MARCHING ORDERS

Keep house, wash your ass, look after yourself, police your area, mind your own, work your business, be on time, take care of your things, uphold your promises, tend to your affairs, watch your back, fulfill your obligations, make your due, and that's just to name a few of the more common marching orders.

At least in this life.

Jeffrey Scott Weisman

CHECKING OUT

Maybe it's because we're so used to people coming and going around here that we don't really notice it anymore, or maybe it's because we don't want to think about it in relation to ourselves too much, or maybe it's because whether it's through the front door or the back door it's inevitable, but for whatever reason, we don't really grieve the loss of anyone around here. Now sure, Cotton was heartbroken over his homeboy Marty getting carted out in a body bag when he got sick not too long ago and Lemme was pissed about Tyler getting iced out in the yard a little while back and High Jinks was bummed when Smitty OD'd from some bunk he scored off some fish, but all in all, we don't think about it too much.

We really don't.

Course, that seems to be true no matter where you are. Sad as that is.

Jeffrey Scott Weisman

A NECESSARY EVIL

Cotton says that you should do what you love and Little Crow says that you should love what you do and Lemme says that love ain't got nothing to do with it and Barbwire says that you should do it for the sake of doing it and Cotter says that none of that matters cause it's simply about making enough money so that you can live.

Personally though, aside from it being a necessary evil, I don't have a clue why you should work. I really, really don't.

PUBLIC OFFENSES

Almost took out some family once in a snowstorm when I lost control of this van I borrowed from a friend so that I could move into a new apartment in Lincolnshire.

Threw a baseball at this kid on my little league team at Courville Junior High when he wasn't looking and broke his nose, the kid's screaming still ringing in my ears.

Shot two packages of bottle rockets right at my sister when we were kids thinking it would be funny to scare her. It wasn't.

Swung around with a bread knife in my hand in the kitchen one afternoon when I wasn't paying a lick of attention and nearly stabbed my ex right in the gut.

Served a huge plate of half-cooked chicken to my girlfriend Carmen when we were living in Bakerville cause I thought it was supposed to be "red in the middle." It wasn't.

Missed my dad's skull by mere inches when my axe head broke off while I was chopping wood for him when we were out camping in Sheffield. Lucky ass bastard too.

And those are only a few that come to mind.

THUNDER CLAPS

There's shouts and yelps and roars and buzzes and cracks and whistles and jabbers and cackles and hoots and hollers and bellows and clanks and stomps and clicks and flushes and bangs and chirps and chimes and hums and coughs and clunks and hacks and sneezes and dings and wails and shrieks and screams and cheers and whoops and boos and snaps and squeals and moans and belches and hiccups and laughs and yaps and farts and rings and yawps and yammers and crunches and hisses and gurgles and clinks and bleeps and blips and beeps and squawks and sniffs and groans and chatter that all crackle in here like thunder claps.

Jeffrey Scott Weisman

And those are only some of the more common ones too.

NOT A CLUE

When I was about thirteen years old, my friend Trevor and I were out in the field behind his house in Branford, just climbing trees, exploring things, hunting for trouble, when we came across this baby bunny lying in this hole in the ground, its back legs broken or something, making these strange squeaking sounds. And after studying it for a moment, Trevor picked it up, petted it a few times, before chucking it on the ground as hard as he could, laughing gleefully.

And then I did the same thing, heaving it with all my might, the bunny paralyzed with shock, before finally dying, after

maybe ten throws onto the ground, bash,
bash, bash.

And I still don't know why we did that. Not
a clue.

A MODUS OPERANDI

Stick to the regs, listen to the bull guards, follow your orders, mind the warden, avoid your conflicts, stay out of trouble, and those are just a few of the more obvious ones.

Course, that's just a good life strategy. No matter where you are.

Jeffrey Scott Weisman

A DEEPER MEANING

Sometimes Lemme will spend the whole day doing nothing but sitting on his bunk playing solitaire against himself, just lining up his cards one after another like his whole life depends on it. And when I asked him once while we were waiting for morning head count to finish up why he did that, he said, "Cause you gotta learn how to lose in order to know how to win."

And honestly, that could be said about everything in life.

TWO SIDES TO THE SAME COIN

They say you're either up or down, winning or losing, ahead or behind, living it up or living it down. That kind of thing, you know? "Coming up roses," Cotter likes to chuckle, opening up one of his care packages from his old lady, while pulling out a jar of shelled peanuts.

But really, it's all just two sides to the same coin. That's what I say at least.

Jeffrey Scott Weisman

SPLITSVILLE

It was a Thursday evening in May, I had been out doing a few errands around town, when I walked into my place and saw my ex sitting on the couch, her bag packed next to her, her arms folded across her chest, clearly waiting for me to come home. "What's up?" I asked, tossing my keys onto the dining room table in the house we rented together at the time.

"Sit down, babe," she said, patting the seat cushion next to her, the look on her mug indescribably serious.

"Okay," I answered, walking over to the couch, the whole time feeling like I was being invited to my own execution, before sitting down next to her. "Something wrong?"

"I've found another man," she simply replied, looking at me, not even a moment's hesitation on her part.

"You what?" I mumbled, not expecting to hear that come out of her maw. "Why?"

And well, to cut to the chase, it turns out that I was a bad person, a bad husband, a bad lover, a bad provider, a bad sperm donor, and that she wanted more out of life from "her Allen," as she so kindly put it, than I could give her.

Now talk about a gut punch. Damn.

Jeffrey Scott Weisman

TEMPLES

Barbwire likes to say, "Your body's your temple," while we're working out in the yard. Course, around here, people treat their temples like complete trash—they shoot whatever they can into them and they shove whatever they can up them and they cram whatever they can get down them and they toss whatever they can into them. Seriously, it's a field day of Sunday worship, if we follow Barbwire's line of thought about your body being a temple and all.

Although that does seem to be true no matter where you are.

BLUEBLOODS

They think they're better than you and that they own you and that they have a right to everything in the world. Clark's one, for example. He walks around acting like he can do whatever he wants, whenever he wants, however he wants by his birthright alone.

It's sick too.

"It's like we're nothing to him," High Jinks will crack when he sees Clark prancing around the block with his commissary bounty. "That entitled fool."

"No shit," I will reply. "Plum insane."

Fucking bluebloods.

Jeffrey Scott Weisman

CAREER CHOICES

Cotton wanted to be a paramedic.

And Lemme wanted to be a high school science teacher.

And High Jinks wanted to be a cop.

And Cotter wanted to be a truck driver.

And Little Crow wanted to be a car salesman.

And Jasper wanted to be an engineer.

And I wanted to be a home appraiser.

Course, those weren't our ultimate choices.

Obviously.

Jeffrey Scott Weisman

BLACK AND WHITE

It'd be really nice if things were black and white. That it was clear as day as to what you should do in this situation and how you should handle that situation and what you should do about this problem, cause then I'd know what to do about Menace's threat again the other day when he passed me in the corridor leading back from my work assignment, saying, "I'm coming for you, fool. Gonna shank your ass. Just a matter of time."

Yeah, that'd be really nice.

LABELED

A baby, a son, a child, a boy, a cousin, a nephew, a grandson, a teen, a student, a buddy, a troublemaker, an employee, a young man, a thief, a sweetheart, a brother, a goof, a goon, a man, a honey, a neighbor, a homie, a nuisance, a threat, a husband, a babe, an asshole, a killer, a monster, an inmate, a friend, a jerk, a cellie, a con, just to name a few.

But I don't think any of them really apply. At least not completely.

Jeffrey Scott Weisman

IN THE SNAP OF A FINGER

I used to think that I had all the time in the world. That tomorrow would never come, that today would never end, that old age was something that happened to other people, that death was a lifetime away. But I couldn't have been more wrong about that, cause the truth is, it's over before it really begins.

"In the snap of a finger," Cotton likes to say, walking in the yard next to me, the clatter of the other voices and the huff of breathing pattering in the air filling my earholes, while snapping his fingers for emphasis.

Now, ain't that a fact.

THE LUCK OF THE DRAW

Lemme has the kind of disposition that lets him tolerate almost anything. And Cotton has the kind of personality that endears him to almost everyone right off the bat. And High Jinks has the kind of physical attributes that impresses almost everyone that ever meets him. And Barbwire has the kind of verbal dexterity that lets him worm his way out of almost anything.

But really, all that's just the luck of the draw.

That's what I say at least.

Jeffrey Scott Weisman

LAST RITES

When my ma died seventeen years back from her Adderall overdose, my ex made me go to her funeral. Made being the operative word there.

And I remember standing in the cemetery in Courville, the November air crisp against my cheeks, my black suit on, my uncle and his wife standing there next to my ex and me, my pa having died from his stroke a year or so before that, my sister and her husband there looking annoyed, my ma's one friend Mrs. Donway there too, the casket being lowered into the ground, listening to this little old priest say, "Lord, deliver her soul from every bond of sin," while thinking, "Good luck with that one, ma."

Damn right I did. Fuck.

Jeffrey Scott Weisman

PULLING STINTS

Some are easy.

Some are hard.

Some are long.

Some are short.

Some are simple.

Some are complicated.

Some are crazy.

Some are sane.

Some make it out.

Most don't.

Jeffrey Scott Weisman

WOLVES

They come out of the woodwork, looking to pounce on you the moment you make any kind of mistake or error. "Like wolves," Lemme says, watching one of them capitalize on a fish getting in the wrong line in the mess hall or some con messing up in school. "Waiting to tear you to shreds in order to lift themselves up."

Damn right they do. It's fucking sick.

OWNED

Cars, trucks, TVs, couches, beds, pants, shoes, shirts, socks, underwear, pajamas, refrigerators, microwaves, coffee makers, dishwashers, freezers, pots, pans, silverware, lamps, rugs, shoes, recliners, boots, razors, combs, toothbrushes, suitcases, ties, watches, bowls, phones, computers, stereos, tables, pillows, blankets, towels, picture frames, posters, drills, wrenches, hammers, screwdrivers, toolboxes, brooms, mops, nicknacks, fans, jackets, shotguns, revolvers, hats, gloves, to name but a few.

And more than once too.

Jeffrey Scott Weisman

ON MY WORD

I figured out what I'm gonna do about Menace. Course, Lemme ain't happy about it in the least. "Just let it go," he said, nearly pleading with me in the mess hall the other day, to be blunt about it. And High Jinks told me to, "think about your good behavior credit," again last night. But it ain't that simple. Your name's all you've got.

Damn right it is.

So just give me some time.

MY TWO CASES

The first was that guy I stabbed in self-defense. Course, the jury didn't totally buy that argument, given the ten puncture wounds and the fact that I fled the scene and all, but it was self-defense. Scout's honor.

And the second was that old man I shot point-blank in the face when I was robbing that credit union in Livingston. Now that one's totally my fault. See, I thought I had the place staked out proper, and that I knew where all the employees were going to be, and that it was going to be an easy in and out deal, but when I went in there, and passed them my note, "Give me the money and I'll give you your life," everything was going fine until that old man walked out from this side office I didn't know about, saw me standing at the teller, and rushed up to me, stammering, "Sir, sir, what are you doing?" And I simply panicked. That's all that can be said about that. I shot him right in the mug.

Damnit.

So those are my two. Just so we're clear.

THE STATUS QUO

Truth be told, maybe some of us aren't meant to live our own lives. That our thoughts about love and happiness and hope and tomorrow are simply illusions meant to haunt us. That's all they are. And that this is all our life is. And that there ain't nothing else.

Tragic as that is.

Jeffrey Scott Weisman

ONE IN A MILLION

The bull guards and the block bosses
and the warden and whatnot all call me
inmate 21354-068, but my name's
Matthew Rylan Stavers. That's what my
ma and pa labeled me at least. While the
other cons like to tag me Switch, since I
have a chance for parole in a few more
years, if I keep to my good time and all.
But really, I prefer lifer, cause that's how
I see myself in the end.

Course, whether I'm in here or not, I'm
just one in a million.

Lifers, that is. Damn.

About the Author

Jeffrey Scott Weisman grew up in the suburbs of Chicago, went to college in the middle of America, went to graduate school in Boulder, Colorado, traveled throughout Europe for a while in his twenties, moved to Portland, Oregon, for several years, and now lives and teaches English in Elgin, Illinois. He writes daily (some of his works include *"The Greatest Place on Earth"* (published by JEF Books, 2021), *The Disposable Nation, Blood Wrath Row, The Puzzle of Joshua Dover, The Tuck Murders, King Edward IV, The Milford Falls Caper, The Empire of Dreams,* and *Cracks in the Sky*).

A Checklist of JEF Titles

* Winners of the Kenneth Patchen Award for the Innovative Novel

JOURNAL OF EXPERIMENTAL FICTION

JEF